I Can Read!™

BEGINNING 1 READING

Dixie

Wins the Race

story by Grace Gilman
pictures by Jacqueline Rogers

HARPER
An Imprint of HarperCollinsPublishers

Dear Parent:
Your child's love of reading starts here!

Every child learns to read in a different way and at his or her own speed. Some go back and forth between reading levels and read favorite books again and again. Others read through each level in order. You can help your young reader improve and become more confident by encouraging his or her own interests and abilities. From books your child reads with you to the first books he or she reads alone, there are I Can Read Books for every stage of reading:

SHARED READING
Basic language, word repetition, and whimsical illustrations, ideal for sharing with your emergent reader

BEGINNING READING
Short sentences, familiar words, and simple concepts for children eager to read on their own

READING WITH HELP
Engaging stories, longer sentences, and language play for developing readers

READING ALONE
Complex plots, challenging vocabulary, and high-interest topics for the independent reader

ADVANCED READING
Short paragraphs, chapters, and exciting themes for the perfect bridge to chapter books

I Can Read Books have introduced children to the joy of reading since 1957. Featuring award-winning authors and illustrators and a fabulous cast of beloved characters, I Can Read Books set the standard for beginning readers.

A lifetime of discovery begins with the magical words "I Can Read!"

Visit www.icanread.com for information
on enriching your child's reading experience.

JAN 1 4 2013

I Can Read Book® is a trademark of HarperCollins Publishers.

Dixie Wins the Race Copyright © 2012 by HarperCollins Publishers. All rights reserved. Manufactured in China. No part of this book may be used or reproduced in any manner whatsoever without written permission except in the case of brief quotations embodied in critical articles and reviews. For information address HarperCollins Children's Books, a division of HarperCollins Publishers, 10 East 53rd Street, New York, NY 10022.
www.icanread.com

Library of Congress catalog card number: 2011945729
ISBN 978-0-06-208618-1 (trade bdg.) —ISBN 978-0-06-208614-3 (pbk.)

12 13 14 15 16   SCP   10 9 8 7 6 5 4 3 2 1   ❖   First Edition

JE READER

Emma loved to run.

Dixie loved to run, too.

"Come on, Dixie," Emma said.

"Come and see my track team run."

Dixie yipped.

She yapped.

Dixie didn't want to watch.

She wanted to run.

Today, Emma was going to run a relay race.

"I will run the last part

of the race," Emma told Dixie.

"You can't run with me.

But you can cheer for me!"

"Be good, Dixie," said Emma.

"Sit. Stay. Cheer."

Dixie sat beside the track to watch.

She wanted to run.

But she had to be good.

She knew what to do.

Sit. Stay. Cheer.

"On your mark!" said the coach.

"Get set! Go!"

The first runners took off!

Each runner carried a stick.

Dixie watched Emma's team.

Her legs shook.

Dixie wanted to run.

She wanted that stick.

The first runner ran one lap.
Then she handed the
stick to the next runner
on the team.

The kids ran fast.

Dixie could run fast, too!

But she had to be good.

Sit. Stay. Cheer.

The second runner passed the stick

and the third runner took off.

Emma lined up.

It was her turn to run.

Dixie stood up to watch.

Emma got the stick.

She ran!

Dixie opened her mouth.

She took a deep breath.

It was time to cheer!

Everyone heard Dixie cheering.

Everyone turned to look at Dixie.

Emma turned, too.

Oh, no!

Emma tripped!

The stick flew out of her hand!

Dixie had to be good.

She had to sit and stay.

But she had to help Emma!

Dixie did not sit.

She did not stay.

Dixie ran to Emma.

She picked up the stick in her teeth,

and she ran!

Dixie ran as fast as she could!

Dixie heard the cheers.

She kept on running.

Dixie saw the finish line.

She kept on running.

Dixie crossed the finish line
with the stick in her teeth!

"Dixie, you did not sit," said Emma.

"You did not stay."

Dixie hung her head.

Emma patted Dixie's head.

"But it's okay," she said.

"Thank you for running to help me."

Emma smiled.

"And Dixie," she said,

"you won the race!"